31 Daily Diversity Thoughts

From Diversity Thoughts to Inclusive Actions

Bestselling Author

DR. SERELDA L. HERBIN, DBF, CDE, DSL, MBA

A GREAT RESOURCE FOR BREAK OUT SESSIONS, SMALL GROUPS, FACILITATIONS, WORKSHOPS, AND TRAINING

Copyright ©2023 by Serelda L. Herbin
31 Daily Diversity Thoughts
From Diversity Thoughts to Inclusive Actions
Dr. Serelda L. Herbin

Visit Dr. Serelda L. Herbin
www.coachingthatcares.com

Connect with Dr. Serelda Herbin
Facebook: @coachingthatcares
Linkedin:
https://www.linkedin.com/in/sereldaherbin

Printed in the United States of America.

All rights reserved under International Copyright Law. Contents and/or cover may not be reproduced in whole or part in any form without the express written consent of the Writer.

Dedication

This body of work is dedicated to every person, every leader, and human being in the world. It is also dedicated to the voiceless, the underrepresented, and marginalized. I also dedicate this book to the fair treatment and inclusion professionals who are continuing to fight the good fight of inclusion and belonging.

Keep making a difference and don't give up!

PAY IT FORWARD BY REACHING BACK

AUTHOR'S NOTE

I love LOVE. I love belonging. I love people. I love connections. I am a Black woman who loves all colors, shades, backgrounds, etc. of people! Period. Why do I begin this way? I will tell you. I am dedicated to convincing different groups of people that we are PEOPLE FIRST. Yes, we all carry a culture. We carry prejudices. We carry racism. We carry hate. We carry apathy. We carry empathy, compassion, and care as well. I wonder what would happen if we led from empathy, understanding, and inclusion versus apathy, arrogance, and exclusion.

This question is still being answered by organizations while cultures are being shaped.

THIS PAGE LEFT BLANK

PART I: EMPATHY IS THE KEY TO UNDERSTANDING

#1: Diversity is not just for black people, women, disabled people, and other minorities.

> *Organizations must include all members and stop thinking diversity is just for historically underserved/marginalized groups. When you exclude one group, you really are functioning in cultural dysfunction.*

INSIGHTS

#2: DIVERSITY, EEO, EO, HR, AND CIVIL RIGHTS ARE NOT SYNONYMOUS.

> *EEO, EO, HR, and Civil Rights all have a part in diversity, but it is not diversity, in and of itself. Take time to learn the difference.*

INSIGHTS

_____
_____
_____
_____
_____
_____
_____

#3: CREATING A DIVERSITY "PROGRAM" IS NOT THE ANSWER.

> *If you still think a diversity "program" is the solution, you are deceived. Diversity is the umbrella that covers your organization. The key is knowing what type of umbrella/covering is setting the cultural tone for your organization.*

INSIGHTS

#4: WHY THE "WHITE PEOPLE" NARRATIVE IS GROWING WEAK.

> *It does not matter what race you are, we are all responsible for our behavior and awareness of what we bring to the table. Most major organizations are run and controlled by "white people"- white men, specifically. This is not about one group winning at the expense of another group losing. Learn the power of working together.*

INSIGHTS

#5: DIVERSITY AND INCLUSION: COUSINS, NOT TWINS.

There are several perspectives of diversity and inclusion but one perspective to note is that diversity and inclusion are NOT the same. Stop interchanging the concepts. Diversity is the floor to begin. Inclusion is how we win!!!

INSIGHTS

#6: YOUR DESCRIPTORS TELL THE REAL STORY OF DIVERSITY.

> *We must begin to look at people as "people" first. Telling me that I am a black author versus an author who happens to be black, or a military officer versus an officer who happens to be a female changes the narrative and perspective of the person. Descriptors matter.*

INSIGHTS

#7: MINORITIES ARE PROFILED BEFORE THEY OPEN THEIR MOUTH.

> *As a woman who happens to be black, my color and my gender speak for me before I open my mouth. I understand this. I know it happens. Do not feed the bias. Break the barrier by showing up, delivering, and producing! That is not being naive. That is being aware.*

INSIGHTS

#8: WHITE PEOPLE ARE JUDGED BASED ON THE COLOR OF THEIR SKIN TOO!

This concept of white people being evil or privileged with arrogance is just as skewed as all black people being animals or ghetto, or all Asian people being the cause of the Corona Virus, or Mexican people not knowing how to speak English. While not all white people are advocates of fairness, many are! Don't pass judgment based on color, but on character!

INSIGHTS

_____
_____
_____
_____
_____
_____
_____

#9: STOP PROFILING AND START TALKING.

We underestimate the power of conversation. Sitting down and having a real talk with someone is one of the most valuable assets in an organization and in building rapport. Take time to do it!

INSIGHTS

#10: FEEDBACK IS A GIFT.

> *If you have never practiced appreciative inquiry, start now. Dig deeper and find out what others think. Empower and elevate the thinking of others. When you do, you shift culture-just like that!*

INSIGHTS

#11: INTEGRATE CULTURAL CAPABILITIES AND NOT BARRIERS OF CONSCIOUS BIAS.

All bias is NOT unconscious. Some people operate very overtly in bias simple because they have found ways to get away with the behavior. If humans can find loopholes to EXCLUDE, we can find loopholes to INCLUDE. It works both ways!

INSIGHTS

_____
_____
_____
_____
_____
_____
_____

#12: DIVERSITY NOT JUST ABOUT DATA. IT IS ABOUT DELIVERY TOO.

There are many failed diversity initiatives around the world. There are many who thought using data would solve the issues. Not. Hiding behind data to address organizational behavior is not the answer. We have data overload and action dehydration. It is time for action!

INSIGHTS

#13: Stop looking at skin and start looking at solutions.

The work will begin when people begin looking at the magnitude of established systems versus the hues of skin color. Be the front runner and start making intentional moves towards a sustainable and inclusive culture.

INSIGHTS

_____
_____
_____
_____
_____
_____
_____

#14: NORMALIZE SAFE AND HEALTHY LANGUAGE.

Dialogue and conversations have become fear-driven moments. The only way to overcome this is understanding we should always approach communication that seeks to understand and not just to respond. Fear paralyzes progress. Engagement propels us!

INSIGHTS

_____
_____
_____
_____
_____
_____
_____

#15: Be an architect of change.

Architects create things and concepts that last. They don't build anything that is not foundationally safe. Yes, risk is always present but, planning and preparation will always mitigate failure. Become true change agent of culture.

INSIGHTS

_____
_____
_____
_____
_____
_____
_____

Dr. Serelda L. Herbin 17

PART II: UNDERSTANDING IS THE KEY TO ACTION

#16: BE MINDFUL OF DIVERSITY REJECTION.

Be mindful of "diversity rejection." All engagements are not receptive ones. Everyone is not happy about the concept of diversity in the workplace. Prepare for rejection but leverage the opposing opinions-they are oftentimes helpful to building sustainable diversity initiatives.

INSIGHTS

#17: ACCEPT THAT NO ONE KNOWS EVERYTHING.

> *Showing up, pretending to know everything, is not healthy or beneficial. It is the quickest way to lose credibility. Being prepared for the work is one thing. Presenting oneself as knowing all the answers are yet another.*

INSIGHTS

#18: BE INTENTIONAL IN CAPTURING GENUINE EXPERIENCES.

Observing behavior in oneself and others is extremely important when building, or rebuilding a culture. We must understand how we SEE NOW to know what we WANT to SEE LATER.

INSIGHTS

_____
_____
_____
_____
_____
_____
_____

#19: POLICY AND RULES CANNOT CHANGE CULTURE.

> *Culture is the engine to the vehicle; strategy and policy is the actual vehicle- it cannot operate without and engine!*
> *Strategy maximized is culture energized!*

INSIGHTS

_____
_____
_____
_____
_____
_____
_____

#20: BE OPEN. BE ADAPTABLE. BE AGILE.

As people and organizations, we must be open, prepared, and ready to be respectful of experiences opposite of our own lived experiences.
It is not always about YOU! Open your aperture!

INSIGHTS

#21: CULTURAL DEXTERITY AND CULTURAL COMPETENCE ARE RUDDERS FOR LEADERS AND EMPLOYEES. IT IS ALMOST IMPOSSIBLE TO LEAD WITHOUT THEM!

> *Developing leaders is less about being "in charge" but more about understanding "the charge" to guide the organizational culture and climate with inclusion and respect-FOR ALL!*

INSIGHTS

_____
_____
_____
_____
_____
_____
_____

#22: ORGANIZATIONS DON'T HAVE COMMUNICATION PROBLEMS. THEY HAVE CONNECTION PROBLEMS.

Organizations have an abundance of communication sources, but seldom find the sweet spot of connection those communication resources for organizational effectiveness. Do not stop at hearing. Seek to connect and

INSIGHTS

_____
_____
_____
_____
_____
_____
_____

#23: DIVERSITY IS PART OF ORGANIZATIONAL HEALTH JUST AS EATING IS PART OF HUMAN HEALTH.

> Anything that's health should grow. This applies to organizations as well. Check your organizational vital signs: recruitment, hiring, promotions, personnel turnover, development, retention, culture- vital organizational nutrients.

INSIGHTS

_____
_____
_____
_____
_____
_____
_____

#24: DIVERSITY PROFESSIONALS DO NOT HAVE TO BE HR OR LEGAL PROFESSIONALS.

Diversity practitioners and champions SHOULD possess various backgrounds. Having a WILLINGNESS to lead culture change is an indication of empathy, understanding, and inclusion.

INSIGHTS

#25: DIVERSITY WORK CANNOT BE DONE ALONE. IT TAKES ALL HANDS ON DECK!

> *The most effective diversity leaders and teams must understand the importance of cross-functional teaming and the value of teaming, internally and externally. Use your networks. Do not burn out!*

INSIGHTS

_____
_____
_____
_____
_____
_____
_____

#26: SEEK TO BUILD PEOPLE WHO WILL CHAMPION INCLUSION AND BELONGING FOR ALL.

Workplace behaviors are formed by EVERYONE, not just leaders. We bring our lived experiences, opinions, biases, presuppositions, etc. to work with us. We must work "beyond ourselves" and seek to create a collaborative, high-performing organization.

INSIGHTS

#27: R.A.T.E. YOUR ENGAGEMENT.

*Everyone has their own individual perspective of diversity. When we R.A.T.E. our engagement, we are simply remaining mindful that everyone is at different levels of understanding diversity awareness. Some need **Refreshers**. Some are gaining **Awareness**. Others are requiring **Training**. Many need overall **Education**.*

INSIGHTS

_____
_____
_____
_____
_____
_____
_____

#28: REINFORCE THE IMPORTANCE OF DIVERSITY THROUGH ACCOUNTABILITY.

Accountability is not about being a behavior police. It is more about modeling behavior that is inclusive, emotionally intelligent and aware of ALL members of an organization. Accountability requires more than activity. It requires sustainability and operationalizing diversity as a mission set.

INSIGHTS

_____
_____
_____
_____
_____
_____
_____

#29: DIVERSITY IS NOT ABOUT QUOTAS, THE ROONEY RULE, DIVERSE HIRES, TOKENISM, OR GENERIC TALENT POOLS.

Organizations and leaders must focus on establishing milestones and a means to track, develop, and assess diversity efforts that enhances representation at ALL LEVELS of the organization.

INSIGHTS

#30: UNDERSTAND THIS: SOME PEOPLE WILL NEVER CHANGE!

Learn to focus on those individuals who are empowered and excited to improve culture and make a positive difference. However, ALWAYS, ALWAYS, ALWAYS create a safe space for all opinions to be heard and considered.
THAT IS TRUE DIVERSITY, EQUITY, INCLUSION, AND ACCESSIBILITY FOR ALL!

INSIGHTS

_____
_____
_____
_____
_____
_____
_____

#31: EVERY POINT OF VIEW MATTERS.

> *Some feel that an organization should be like a melting pot. Others think it is like a mixed salad. Others feels organizations are like a bag of Skittles, while others feel it should be like akin to a bowl of gumbo. It is all a matter of perspective. Inclusion and Belonging is the key!*

INSIGHTS

_____
_____
_____
_____
_____
_____
_____

OTHER BOOKS

FOR BOOKING OR BULK BOOK ORDERS,
CONTACT US:
INFO@COACHINGTHATCARES.COM

Made in the USA
Middletown, DE
22 February 2026

28545876R00024